I0526926

MANHATTAN GHOST

Story:
Philippe WARD

Photos:
Mickaël LAGUERRE

Translation:
Brian Stableford

BLACK COAT PRESS

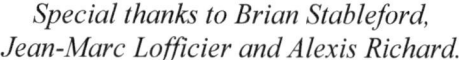

Special thanks to Brian Stableford,
Jean-Marc Lofficier and Alexis Richard.

© 2014 Philippe Ward & Mickaël Laguerre. Couverture © 2014 Mickaël Laguerre. ISBN 978-1-61227-329-7. First Printing. September 2014. Published by Black Coat Press, an imprint of Hollywood Comics.com, LLC, P.O. Box 17270, Encino, CA 91416. All rights reserved.
Except for review purposes, no part of this book may be reproduced or transmitted in any form or by any means, electronic or mechanical, including photocopying, recording, or by any information storage and retrieval system, without permission in writing from the publisher.
The stories and characters depicted in this novel are entirely fictional. Printed in the United States of America.

The streets of New York
A maze made of iron and stone.
A labyrinth complete,
With edges that cut through the bone.

They come by the millions,
The hipster, the prince and the clown.
They come 'cause they know that
Something's going down…
On the streets of New York.

Willie Nile, *On the Streets of New York.*

On the streets of New York...

The streets of New York: Lisa Kilpatrick knew them by heart; she was pure New Yorker, born thirty-four years before at Lenox Hill Hospital in the heart of the Upper East Side, and had lived ever since in that city, which she adored more than anything else. Her only infidelities to New York had been scholarly excursions to Washington, Boston or Providence and a wedding trip to Las Vegas, which had not brought her happiness, because she had got divorced two years later, for various reasons.

Dressed in jeans and a black leather jacket she emerged from the Fourteenth Street subway station. She didn't take the trouble to get her bearings and walked at a fast pace toward the Starbuck's on Eighth Avenue. In spite of being five foot nine and having long red hair—a legacy of her Irish ancestry—she went unnoticed in New York. No one turned round to look at her as if she were some kind of curious animal, because people were in too much of a hurry here, to absorbed to pay attention to others—except for tourists, whom they helped when they saw them looking at a city map. Lisa adored the well-tempered character of the city, which never gave anything because it as too self-obsessed. Lisa loved it in spite of its individualism and its frantic quest for green bills. New York was astir for twenty-four hours out of twenty-four, seven days a week, three hundred and sixty-five days a year: a veritable perpetual motion.

Lisa adjusted the earpieces of her i-phone and murmured the words to Willie Nile's *Streets of New York*. Two joggers went past her at a run while a bunch of suits drank their coffee on the way to their bank while discussing the direction of the Dow. She went into Starbuck's, switched off her phone and waited patiently for her turn, like any New Yorker. It would never have occurred to her to jump the queue. She ordered a double espresso and when it was handed to her she went to sit down on a stool at the window overlooking the street. She pressed *play*. Then she added sugar to her cup and her gaze wandered out into the street.

Her day's work finished, she could breathe before attacking the next, which would be totally different. Willie Nile gave way to Harry Belafonte's *New York Taxi*. As if to respond to the song, a whole fleet of yellow cabs passed before her in an uninterrupted file, as if the streets of New York belonged to them and they had expelled all the other vehicles: another powerful symbol of New York, which could not be confused with other cars.

Lisa drank her coffee, sniffing the odor that reigned in Starbuck's. She savored the moment of tranquility that she accorded herself: a rare interval in her crazy life. She looked at her watch. Three minutes past eight; she still had time before tackling her second job, about half an hour to take advantage of the calm.

She took another sip, closed her eyes, and suddenly opened them with a start. She spilled the coffee on the table. The naked body of a young woman had just imposed itself on her mind. She tried to chase away the vision, but nothing worked. She thought about the basketball game she had watched the day before, but it did no good. She closed her eyes again, concentrated on Harry Belafonte's voice and imagined all the cabs in New York rolling along the immense avenues, but nothing worked. The song was no more than a distant murmur and the taxis no longer existed for her. The young woman's bruised face remained engraved in her consciousness.

Lisa understood that she would not be able to get rid of it so easily. Fourteen years in the New York Police left indelible traces. Fourteen years of seeing corpses, and she had never gotten used to it. Not to mention the interrogations of murderers, thieves and other monsters engendered by the city. Fourteen years without any veritable respite, always fighting crime without any hope of winning.

Thanks to the pressure of the hierarchy and the politicians, who wanted New York to be a safe metropolis, a city where tourists could travel the subway by night without risk of aggression, the police had almost got there after fourteen years; crime had quit Manhattan in large measure to take refuge in the other boroughs. The mayor was content with his political security and was now able to attack the dangers of fizzy drinks and obesity—a scourge more difficult to eradicate than the Mafia. And yet, the murders kept flowing in the Big Apple, like the one committed the day before, whose investigation had been assigned to her. A woman of about twenty, a beautiful blonde, doubtless originally from Eastern Europe, surely a prostitute, had been savagely beaten to death.

Given the violence of the blows landed on the face and the body, Lisa had originally bet on a dissatisfied customer—except that on the woman's belly, two buildings had been painted in an abstract fashion, side by side, with a sun above them, just below her breasts, and a red dot in the center of the star.

Lisa had understood that the killer had struck at that exact spot. She didn't know whether the design had been there before the murder or whether it was the killer's work. Depending on the answer to that question, her investigation might take on different complexions. She was waiting for the results of the autopsy and the initial enquiries, which her colleagues would communicate to her in the morning. Then she would know whether she had to plunge into the murky world of prostitution or, worse, into a sick mind.

This evening, though, she didn't want to think about the young woman or her murderer. That wouldn't be easy, but she had to try.

Lisa had joined the police out of necessity, never having had a feeling or vocation for it. She was descended from a long line of cops, though, ever since an ancestor had disembarked on Staten Island at the end of the nineteenth century. He had found a place in the bosom of the New York Police thanks to an Irish cousin; then her grandfather and father had followed the same path: a path that she had never envisaged during her childhood. Since she was very small her dream had been music, from the day that her mother had enrolled her in piano lessons at the age of nine. For ten years she had continued her apprenticeship in that instrument, and then had taken singing lessons while pursuing her studies and playing the organ in church every Sunday.

At the age of twenty she had applied to Julliard. After an audition, she had been accepted, and that had been the best day of her life. Unfortunately, the worst day of her life had arrived the following week. Some little bitch high on crack had fatally stabbed her father, a passionate cop, when he had just arrested her after a sordid summing. The addict had put an end to her career as a musician and singer. An only child, she had been left with her mother, who had never worked, obliged to assume responsibility for the household, medical insurance and all the rest.

Money was still the sinew of New York and all Americans; without it, life threw you out unceremoniously. Without it, the doors of Julliard were definitively closed to her. Her father had always encouraged her on that path and supported her in her ambition to get into the world of music. He had economized in order to pay for her studies, but from one day to the next Lisa's life had fallen apart. She had had to get a job in order to eat. Fortunately, her father's friends had succeeded in getting her into the police force. It was rather inglorious to get in by means of pull, but she hadn't refused that aid.

She had begun at the bottom of the ladder, in traffic; then, gradually, she had risen through the ranks competitively, getting her revenge on life, eventually obtaining that of Lieutenant. In the beginning, her job had remained a simple meal ticket, to finish paying off her mother's house, and her own rent. As the years went by, though, she had allowed herself to be captured by her work, to become a true cop, who never let up in any of her investigations. At her precinct, her superiors considered her to have a stronger itch than many of her colleagues. The hardest thing for her was to be in close proximity with death; she had never gotten used to it and never would. The other cops regarded death with disdain, but not her. For the moment, her mental health was holding up, but she was afraid of sinking into alcoholism, as many cops did.

Slowly, her passion for music had been diluted, to become a vague memory about which she no longer wanted to think. She had definitively drawn a line under her artistic ambitions. She sometimes experienced regrets, but she no longer thought about that life in music. She had married a policeman from another precinct but the job had broken the couple up—again. The divorce papers had been a pure formality. They had parted as good friends and still saw one another from time to time. For five years she had lived alone in an apartment in Chelsea; the rent cost her a small fortune, but she hadn't wanted to leave Manhattan. Sometimes, a man spent a night or two in her bed, rarely more. Afterwards, she plunged back into the investigations that had become her life.

Then, one day, a year ago, for her thirty-third birthday, her mother had taken her to a restaurant in Little Italy. At the end of the meal, she had got up, taken her by the hand to drag her to an upright piano standing in a corner of the room, and launched into a "Happy birthday to you." It was her present.

Lisa had nearly laughed at the incongruity of the gift, but she had held back on seeing the tears running down her mother's cheeks. She had sat down in front of the piano. For a moment, the thought of getting up get up and leaving the restaurant had crossed her mind, but she had abandoned the idea, because she suspected that her mother must have saved up a dollar at a time for years to buy her the piano. She had swallowed her rage and lifted the lid.

The sensations had returned of their own accord. Lisa had played pieces by Chopin and Mozart before changing tack with the Beatles and Elton John, without noticing the time passing, and finishing up with John Lennon's *Imagine*—which, to her great surprise, she had sung.

In the beginning, her mother had been her only audience—or, rather, admirer—but as one piece followed another the conversations in the restaurant had died away, customers had come over to the piano after settling the check and the waiters had paused to listen. After having played the last chords of *Imagine* she had got up and dissolved in tears in her mother's arms, and had thanked her, awkwardly wiping her cheeks. When she had quit her mother's arms she had looked at the piano, wondering what to do with it. After a moment's reflection she had made her decision; she would not refuse the gift.

The hardest thing was getting it up to her third floor apartment. Her mother had bought it in a store next door to the restaurant and had the idea of making a gift of it there without thinking about the next step. Lisa had asked some of her colleagues, burly guys, to help her, and they had all accepted without scowling. She had hired a truck to transport it.

Several times she had thought she would see it smashed at the bottom of the stairwell, but it had finally arrived in good condition. She had installed it against the wall in the interior hallway, and warned her neighbors that there was a risk that she might play it and make a noise, but they had all reassured her, saying that they wouldn't complain as long as here weren't too many bum notes. She had told them she would do her best.

For a week, she hadn't touched it. When she got back from the precinct, exhausted by her day or night, she hadn't had the energy to play. In any case, a question had pricked her consciousness: play what, and for whom? For herself? For the neighbors? For her mother? With regard to the instrument, she had felt a mixture of excitement and rage. It represented simultaneously everything that she loved and the catastrophe of her life: the catastrophe of having been missed out on a great career, or at least of making a living from her passion. The gift had been a true poisoned chalice, because it reminded her every day of what she might have been and what she had become.

And brutally, the love of music had replaced the anger. After a difficult day in which she had not persuaded a rapist to confess and his lawyer, from a big firm, had torn her investigation apart, she had fallen upon her piano to play jazz tunes, and even to let her imagination wander. On the following days, she had played for a quarter of an hour. She had bought some scores, and the pleasure had gradually returned. She had understood that, even if she had drawn a line under her career, it had been a serious mistake to abandon the piano and singing.

After playing, she had started to sing. In the beginning, it had been bad; her hoarse, jerky voice had lost its timbre. But Lisa had forced herself to recover the tonality she had had at twenty.

Those moments soothed her and made her forget the harshness of her métier. Throughout those minutes, she no longer thought about corpses, killers and all the filth she cleaned up. All that vanished temporarily from her mind,

One evening, when she was drinking a Brooklyn beer in a baron Ninth Avenue with her colleagues, she had got up without thinking about it to go over to a piano that was waiting desperately for someone to want to play it. She completely ignored the comments that the regulars were doubtless about to make and played with feeling. After the first piece, a Chopin nocturne, she attacked Willie Nile's *Streets of New York*, and started to sing, the words coming of their own accord. When she had finished everyone there applauded wildly and demanded another song. She had launched into the standard *New York, New York* immortalized by Frank Sinatra and Lisa Minnelli, among others. The power of her voice had filled the bar and she had ended the song, which was almost her life, breathless. Her colleague has asked for an encore, but she had refused, returning to her seat to finish her beer.

The owner of the bar had come over to see her, to offer her a half-hour spot one evening a week, to begin whenever she liked. Lisa burst out laughing and refused point blank. She couldn't imagine a New York police lieutenant singing in a bar. Her colleagues had encouraged her to accept, though, singing being better than playing bodyguard or detective to round out the end of the month, supplementing the derisory salary of a New York cop.

She said that she would think about it and give her answer the next day. All night her mind had been seething. In the past, she had reasoned with herself that should would never have become a star, and now she laughed at the notion—but the idea of taking up music again, of playing before a small audience, even if some of them were there for the alcohol and trawling for dates, appealed to her. At least music would have a place in her life again, a place that it would never have to quit. By dawn, her decision was irrevocable; she accepted the offer, paying little attention to the terms the bar owner was offering. Even if it wouldn't bring her much financially, it would be good for her mental health. To be able to escape from work, even for half an hour a week, was priceless.

So, from that day on, one evening a week, depending on her shifts and her fatigue, physical as well as mental, she played in the bar, and people increasingly came to listen to her. Word of mouth functioned at full tilt. Articles in blogs talked about her agility and praised her voice and sense of rhythm. She appreciated all the encouragement, but avoided getting big-headed.

She had progressively adapted her repertoire in accordance with her musical tastes and now mostly sang songs about New York. The city had attracted numerous composers in various genres: jazz, rock, rap, blues and others. She was spoiled for choice in digging into the almost infinite list.

An ambulance siren brought her back to reality. Another noise typical of the city, she thought. Reviewing her past had succeeded in chasing away the image of the dead woman. She finished her coffee, which had gone cold, and looked at her watch. She still had time in hand, and even if she were a few minutes late it would not be catastrophic. The audience wouldn't break up the bar, and lateness was one of the prerogatives of artistes.

She threw the paper cup into the trash and quit the Starbuck's. She walked unhurriedly to the intersection between Eighth Avenue and Fourteenth Street, where she waited for the light to turn green in order to cross. She noticed a crowd gathering on the far side. She raised her eyebrows, her cop's instinct immediately getting the upper hand. She crossed the avenue and joined a hundred people who had paused on the sidewalk, staring at the end of the street. She noticed that they were all carrying cameras.

She looked around for cops. There were two on the other side of the street, a stony-faced veteran with a pot belly and a young one who had to be fresh out of the academy. Two more in the middle of the avenue were directing the traffic and a fifth as moving on passers-by who were aggregating. The crowd seemed tranquil—no shouting, no slogans, no sudden movements, no banners displaying demands, as happened from time to time in New York—even though a few people where now encroaching on the streets and beginning to hold up traffic.

Lisa could not understand the presence of the multitude. She thought some star might be in the neighborhood—Chelsea was famous for its art galleries, files of models in fashion shows and young stylists launching their careers—but that was inconclusive, just a hypothesis that explained the cameras.

She took out her police badge and went over to one of the photographers.

"Lieutenant Kilpatrick, NYPD," she snapped, in a harsh voice. "What's going on?"

The man raised his eyebrows and stared at the badge. His face went pale. "I'm not doing anything," he said, in a tremulous voice. "I'm waiting for the sun, like everyone else."

It was Lisa's turn to look at him with surprise; it wasn't a response she had expected. "What sun?" she asked, dryly.

She immediately realized the absurdity of the question, but the photographer didn't seem to notice it.

"It's the day of the Manhattanhenge," he said. "In three minutes time, the setting sun will be exactly in the middle of Fourteenth Street, in a perfect western alignment."

The smile returned to Lisa's face. A simple gathering to photograph a rare New York phenomenon: everything was normal, nothing to get excited about. Memories came back to mind. The design of the streets of Manhattan dated back to 1811, and respected the natural axis of the island—except that there was a slight displacement, because that axis was inclined by 29° from the vertical, so that twenty-two days before the summer solstice, the sun set in the axis of the horizontal streets.

"It's called that in honor of Stonehenge," the photographer added. "All the cities in the world have streets and sunsets, but New York is the only one to be furrowed by symmetrical streets bordered by immutable giants. You'll see—it's a totally beautiful spectacle, especially today, because the sky is so clear."

Lisa thanked him with a nod of the head. She decided to stay. A few minutes more was nothing; she could allow herself that.

"There it is!" howled a voice.

Immediately, the photographers took up their positions, their eyes glued to the screens of their apparatus. Slowly, like a star who knows that her fans are waiting for her, the sun advanced at her own pace between the rows of skyscrapers. The orange-tinted sky surrounded her.

Insensible to the charm of the spectacle, a policeman howled at a group of photographers squatting in the street: "Get away, or I'll take you in!"

They took a few more pictures before leaving the spot and returning to the sidewalk. Lisa knew that the cop would have carried out his threat if they hadn't obeyed.

Finally, the sun arrived in the middle of the street.

Lisa looked at it, and was immediately dazzled. She put her hand over her eyes and lost her balance slightly. She succeeded in supporting herself against the wall of a building.

When she opened her eyes, everything was black. She nearly howled that she was blind, but she closed her eyes again and calmed her hectic heartbeat. She opened her eyes for a second time. The color orange had replaced the obscurity and sight gradually came back. She noticed that there were fewer people about than before she had been dazzled. The crowd had thinned out and the sun had disappeared from the street. The photographers and sensation-seekers had gone.

Here malaise must, therefore, have lasted several minutes, even though it had seemed to be a matter of seconds. She looked at her watch, which confirmed, to her amazement, that her daze had hasted less than a minute. And yet, all the photographers had disappeared.

She waited for her heart to resume a normal rhythm before deciding to go to the bar. Now she was going to be late.

"Hello, Lisa."

The young woman turned round abruptly, surprised to be greeted like that in this neighborhood.

"Peter! What are you doing here?"

She caught herself up suddenly, conscious of the incongruity of the question. Peter Monaghan had died three years before of a metastasized cancer, due to overwork, alcohol and, most of all, cigarette abuse. And he was standing facing her, in the blue costume in which Lisa had always known him. His shoulders were more stooped and his face paler than she remembered him. He smiled at her.

"You look resplendent, as ever."

Lisa searched for words, but couldn't find any. Peter raised his hand and a taxi immediately stopped. He opened the door and indicated the interior of the vehicle to Lisa. She was still incapable of speech.

"Where to?" asked the driver, with a broad smile.

Lisa was surprised to see a white face; it had been years since she had taken a cab driven by a white man.

"Madison Square Garden," said Peter.

"You got it," said the man, turning round.

The taxi cabs drive me crazy
How come dey always leaving me
Oh yes the young man drive away.
Quick quick when he hear me say
One twenty-fifth and Lenox please
Don't you know
The taxi gone with the breeze
Sixteen miles I walk, walk, walk, walk
Waiting on a taxi here in New York.

Harry Belafonte, *New York Taxi.*

"I owe you an explanation," said Peter, taking Lisa's hand.

She didn't reply immediately; she looked out of the window to give herself a moment to think. Eighth Avenue seemed deserted. No matter what time of day or night was, though, there were always people about. Even the food trucks seemed to have vanished. She was dreaming; otherwise, it was impossible. She cleared her throat and turned toward her father's friend. Peter guessed what she as thinking and smiled.

"No, you're not dreaming, and I really am dead. You're the one who's my phantom."

"If I'm not dreaming," said Lisa, loudly, "and if you're dead, then I must be died too. A road-hog swerved to avoid the photographers, knocked me down and killed me on the spot. You've come to welcome me as the family's oldest friend. But instead of walking down a white tunnel, we're taking a yellow taxi along Eighth Avenue toward Madison Square Garden, which must be the door to paradise…or purgatory."

Peter's smile broadened.

"Excellent deduction, worthy of the cop you are—but you're wrong. You're not dreaming, I'm dead and you're alive.

Lisa darted an impatient glance at him, her expression darkening.

"Explain, then, instead of mocking me."

"Promise me not to interrupt until I've finished. Afterwards you can ask all the questions you want—but it's possible that I won't have the answers."

Lisa shook her head, while the taxi threaded a path through the rare vehicles. Peter looked straight ahead, and began.

"You're still in New York but on another plane. Here, there are only dead people—or rather, their phantoms. We live in this world because our deaths were brutal: murders, suicides, violent or whatever. None of the people you see died of old age in their beds."

He paused momentarily. Lisa bit her lip in order not to say anything.

"Don't ask me why," Peter continued, without paying any heed to the young woman's disturbance. "I don't know. When I died I found myself on Twentieth Street and another cop was waiting for me to explain it. The dead are more welcoming than the living. As you can see, New York is still New York; I live in my own place, but alone, without my wife and two daughters. I wear the same uniform as I did before dying; it never gets dirty. I spend my days walking and talking. I've never talked so much."

He paused again. Lisa couldn't help saying: "And this will go on for a long time?"

Peter laughed briefly.

"No idea. When I arrived in this world my mentor asked me whether I wanted to stay in New York or go to another city. I told him that I couldn't see myself living anywhere but here. As I told you, there's a heap of things I don't know. There are rules, and I understand some of them, but not much."

He paused again, and went on: "I know who you're thinking about. Your father."

Lisa nodded her head affirmatively. She dared not ask the question, so fearful was she of the reply. Whether she saw her father or not, the result would be the same: sadness.

"Your father isn't in New York," said Peter, calmly.

"That doesn't surprise me," said Lisa, in a relieved tone. "He always said this city was his hell."

"I don't even know whether he's in another city, or elsewhere."

"Elsewhere?"

"Yes, when our period of purgatory is over, we leave for elsewhere, but no one knows what it is, because no one's ever come back to describe it."

Thousands of questions were jostling in Lisa's head, but she kept them to herself; later, there would be a better time to ask them.

"And where do I fit in?" she asked, turning toward her father's friend.

"We need you. You have to help us find John Lennon's murderer."

Lisa couldn't help laughing.

"Everybody knows that. It was Mark Chapman, and so far as I know, he's still in Attica. All his requests for parole have been turned down."

Peter shook his head, with a slight wry smile. "I know, but you're forgetting that you're no longer in your world.

Mechanically, Lisa put her hand on Peter's arm, but encountered no resistance and found it on the seat. The policeman smiled at her.

"You can touch objects but not phantoms. Likewise, we can touch objects—the proof is driving the cab—but not the living. Don't ask me why; I don't know. You soon get used to it."

"Okay—so why am I here?"

"John Lennon disappeared the day before yesterday," he said. "And that worries us, a great deal."

"I don't understand," said Lisa. "I'm completely lost."

"Who wouldn't be? I'm sorry to rush you, but I really do need you. *We* need you."

"To find the murderer of John Lennon's phantom?" she said, sarcastically.

Peter replied in a soft voice that Lisa didn't recognize: "You've got it."

"Not at all. For one thing, a phantom can die?"

"Exactly—he can't. To put it simply, the day we finish our stint in this purgatory, a force pushes us toward a door. Here, in New York, it's at the end of the Brooklyn Bridge. We know that our time is done, we go through the door, and game over."

"And afterwards?"

"Afterwards…as I said, no one's ever come back."

A slight grimace appeared on Lisa's face; new questions were bubbling up in her mind, but she decided to set them aside and accept the situation as it was.

"We're here," said the cab driver, pulling up outside Madison Square Garden.

"The worst of it is that you only have one night to help us. Tomorrow morning, the Manhattanhenge will be over, and you'll find yourself back in the land of the living."

Lisa uttered a sigh of relief; for a moment she had thought that she would find herself definitively trapped in this world. She opened the door and got out. She really was in her New York, but it lacked the crowds, the people in a hurry, the traffic, and even the odors of food and gasoline—not to mention the sound of ambulances.

Peter made a sign inviting her to follow him and headed for the entrance to the immense mythic hall that had seen all the world's great artistes file though, and basketball and hockey games, and boxing matches. The young woman almost reminded him that he hadn't paid for the cab—but money must no longer have any value in this world.

J'ai rêvé New York, New York City sur Hudson.
Babylone, tu te shootes et tu rêves
Babylone, tu fumes trop et tu crèves.
Babylone, tu exploseras sur un graffiti de New York!
Quand il pleut des cordes - Roule en Ford
Si tu veux faire mac – Roule en Cadillac
Si tu veux faire chic – Roule en Buick
Si tu Rockfeller - Roule en Chrysler
J'ai rêvé New York, New York City sur Hudson.

Yves Simon, *J'ai rêvé New York*

[I've dreamed of New York, New York City on the Hudson
Babylon, you shoot up and you dream
Babylon, you smoke too much and you die.
Babylon, you'll explode in the graffiti of New York!
When it's raining stair-rods, drive a Ford
If you want to pick up a whore, drive a Cadillac
If you want to put on the style, drive a Buick
If you're Rockefeller, drive a Chrysler.
I've dreamed of New York, New York City on the Hudson

Yves Simon, *I've dreamed of New York*.]

They went into the immense hall, where Lisa had often accompanied her father to see the Knicks play basketball. The Garden, as New Yorkers call it, is on Seventh Avenue between Thirty-First and Thirty-Third Street, near Penn Station—but before it was there, there were three other Gardens. New York was a city that shifted, that didn't stay in the same place.

"Suppose you explain now," said Lisa, as she walked into the gigantic hall.

"This is where it happened. Every year, for the summer solstice, a big concert is put on by the dead artists for all the phantoms. This year, John Lennon was on charge of the supervision: choosing the performers, the songs, the choreography; he was the mastermind. The day before yesterday he was on stage, at the piano, in front of two hundred people, and he suddenly evaporated. No one's seen him since."

Lisa couldn't help laughing, nervously. "And you want me to find him."

"No—to find the person who worked the trick. You don't understand: if someone can kill a phantom, we're all doomed. And we won't be able to reach what some think of as paradise—or else what's the point of the years spent languishing here? You can't imagine our suffering, and I wouldn't want you to."

"But why don't you investigate? Why come to fetch me? Don't tell me that you're the only cop haunting New York?"

"Of course not—there are a lot of us, although not as many as those we've arrested—but we're all on the list of suspects. That's why I suggested bringing you here."

"And I have ten hours to solve this puzzle?"

"Yes—even less now."

"You really have confidence in me. What's more, I suppose there isn't any evidence, no clues?"

"Yes I have confidence in you, and yes, we aren't in *C.S.I. New York*. You're going to have to rely entirely on your instincts as a cop."

Suddenly, a man appeared in front of them: not very tall, his black hair unkempt, a little black moustache striping an emaciated visage.

"Monaghan, I told you that it wasn't worth the trouble of bringing one of the living over to us. There's no need. I'll find the guilty party without any need for external help."

Peter's face set firm. "We discussed it Mr. Poe, and the decision was unanimous."

"We'll see the result," said the little man, going away—not without darting a glance of hated at Lisa.

"That's Edgar Allan Poe?" asked Lisa, incredulously.

"In person. When he heard about Lennon's disappearance he leapt at the chance, telling everyone that he'd find the murderer, that he was the greatest detective in the city."

"Which might make him a suspect."

"No, he wasn't there. You can strike him off our list."

"First, I'd have to have a list. For the moment, I don't."

Peter opened a door and they arrived in the arena, which was far from full. But there were also people on the terraces facing the stage. Lisa looked at the people, who were wandering around without paying the slightest attention to her. Peter guided her toward the stage, which as plunged in semi-darkness.

"Let's begin at the beginning," said Lisa. "The place where he disappeared."

"Right in front of you. Lennon was sitting at his white piano playing *Instant Karma*. There were a hundred people watching the rehearsal. Suddenly, a blinding light sprang from a spotlight that had exploded, followed by another. When people opened their eyes, Lennon had disappeared, leaving behind a puff of gray smoke. Several musicians ran toward him, but there was nothing but the smoke rising from the stool where he'd been sitting."

"What if it were a simple accident, a combination of light and products?"

"That would be too convenient, too easy. Anyway, I told you, phantoms never die—except on Brooklyn Bridge, when their time comes, and I'm not even sure about that."

"All right, let's work on that assumption. Now, what about motive? Why did it happen to Lennon? Did he have enemies among the phantoms?"

"Our world resembles that of the living: jealousy, scorn and hatred are its common currency. But we can't kill one another. I can stab someone, put thirty bullets in his body, but nothing happens. No blood no pain. As I told you, it isn't paradise. We don't eat, we don't make love, we don't drink, we don't smoke, we don't take drugs. Artists continue to paint, write, sing—they always have an audience. And yet…."

"That doesn't tell me who might want to kill Lennon. Who decided that he would organize the concert?"

"A committee of musicians chooses, collectively. Every year it's someone different."

"Let's begin with them. Is there anyone else who wanted to be the boss this year?"

"I'll ask."

At that moment a spotlight came on and lit up the stage. Lisa was nonplussed, incapable of pronouncing a single word.

Under that unique beam of light, surrounded by obscurity, stood a woman of incendiary beauty. Lisa recognized hr immediately. She had not been born when the woman had died, but her face and her figure still haunted all memories.

Silence abruptly fell in the hall. Notes were heard, and then it was the turn of the voice, soft and sensual, to take up the baton of the physical. Images of another Madison Square Garden, another stage and another song came to Lisa's mind. It was a hymn for the most powerful man in the world, for his birthday.

"She'll remain beautiful forever," said Peter, who was also fascinated. "John Lennon chose her to be the top of the bill at his show."

Lisa did not know what to say. Marilyn Monroe was singing, and she could not do anything but listen to her and look at her, even if she was only a phantom. By her mere presence, she had succeeded in extinguishing all conversations.

"Get out! Make way for new blood."

The gravelly voice had come from behind Lisa, who turned round immediately. A young man clad in a holed T-shirt ornamented with a swastika and ripped jeans advanced along the aisle and continued to shout loudly. Beside him, an utterly hysterical young woman was howling in unison.

"Yeah, out with the old. Down the toilet, make way for the young. We're fed up with this old clinker music."

Voices rose up on the terraces telling the couple to shut up, who continued more loudly, encouraged by the jeers and insulting gibes that rained down upon them.

"You can start with them," said Peter. "Sid and Nancy."

"She doesn't hold it against him that he killed her?" said Lisa, remembering their history.

Sid Vicious and Nancy Spungen: an accursed couple. After leaving the punk rock band the Sex Pistols, Sid had plunged into heroin, initiated by Nancy. In October 1978, in one of the most famous hotels in New York, the Chelsea Hotel, in which Arthur C. Clarke had written *2001: A Space Odyssey*, the New York Police had discovered Nancy's lifeless body, stabbed. A well-paid lawyer had succeeded in persuading them to swallow a story about dealers. Sid had been released but had sunk even further into addiction. Two months later he had died, the victim of an overdose.

"No, they're always together, wandering around New York howling. If you want to interrogate them, I wish you luck."

Lisa shrugged her shoulders and stared at the two young punks, who were heading for the stage under the horrified gaze of Marilyn Monroe, who retreated. Several phantoms tried to stop them, bit none succeeded. Sid Vicious arrived at his goal, installed himself in front of the audience and sang *My Way* in his hoarse voice, to the boos of the immense majority of those present. Only a small group of about ten encouraged him to continue.

"You really think they'll answer questions from a cop who can no longer take any action against them?" asked Lisa. "Don't forget I can't do anything to them—they're already dead. No, I don't think they killed Lennon."

"When they were alive, though, Sid Vicious was known for his brutality."

"Yes, but not for his intelligence. Whoever killed Lennon was clever. If I accept your hypothesis, he's found a radical means of eliminating phantoms. In fact, have there been any other disappearances before or since?"

"Not to my knowledge."

"Let's go look at the crime scene."

Peter led her on to the stage, where Sid Vicious was continuing to massacre the song. He showed her where Lennon had been sitting and then pointed to the place on the ceiling where the two spotlights were located.

"Good. Try to find out whether other musicians were against the choice of Lennon, while I take one last look around, in case I've overlooked something important."

Lisa examined the location carefully, but there was nothing interesting to see, and she had no technical equipment to pick up trace evidence. In any case, the phantoms didn't leave traces. She understood that she was on the wrong track. She could forget about technology; she had to rely on her cop's instinct; that was all she had. She had no idea how she could resolve the affair.

"I have a few names," Peter said, as he rejoined her.

"Are they in the hall."

"No, in the subway."

"So much the better. Let's get out of here—I can't stand hearing him belching any longer. If he weren't dead, I think I'd strangle him myself."

Peter drew her into the wings in order to avoid going through the arena. They were going past several people who nodded to Peter when a suave voice spoke behind them: "Wait a second, Mr. Monaghan."

They turned round. Marilyn was walking toward them, taking small steps because of her figure-hugging dress. "Is this the lady you've brought from the world of the living?" she asked, smiling at Lisa.

"Yes," said Peter. "She's the daughter of one of my colleagues. She works for the NYPD."

"You're going to get him back?"

Lisa didn't know what to say; she could not get over being face to face with the woman who had fascinated thousands of men, and who, fifty years after her death was still one of the greatest symbols of fatal beauty.

"I hope so," she said, timidly.

"You must," murmured Marilyn, in her soft voice. "He's so nice, and he's the best musician in the world."

"Let him die! He has no business being here—he's a filthy Englishman who's disfigured our music. I died too soon to show him what I was capable of."

The voice had come from behind Lisa. She turned round and saw a rather small black woman wearing long black gloves that hid her forearms. She was dressed in a simple black dress and her hair was decorated with gardenias. The most striking thing about her, however, was the hatred she was spitting in Marilyn Monroe's face.

"And you get back to Los Angeles—you don't have anything to do here. New York's the city of jazz, not soup."

Peter took the woman by the arm and drew her into the wings, but she struggled and kicked, howling: "Dirty cops—you ruined my life and you're still at it. At least here you can't put me in prison."

The couple disappeared into the corridor, but the woman's cries were still cursing English musicians who stole the thunder of real singers.

"I'm going to continue the rehearsal, if I can," said Marilyn. "Thanks for your help."

Lisa wanted to ask her who the jealous woman was, but Marilyn had already turned her back. She watched her head for the stage, feeling a twinge of jealousy herself. She tried to sum up the situation. She set aside her questions about the world of phantoms; she ought not to be distracted by that aspect of the problem. She knew that she undoubtedly wouldn't get answers to many of hr questions. She had to concentrate on the essential matter: finding John Lennon. She wandered along the corridor, looking at the posters of all the events that had been staged at Madison Square Garden. She paused in front of a poster for the John Lennon concert in 1972, and those for Elvis, Frank Sinatra and Bob Dylan. Then it was the turn of the Knicks basketball teams and the Rangers ice-hockey teams. She examined all the stars who had sung, danced and played on that stage.

"Sorry," murmured Peter, coming back.

"Who was that?" I asked Lisa. "I thought I recognized her."

"Billie Holiday."

"Lady Day! The greatest jazz singer of all. I'd never have recognized her."

"Even among phantoms thirty years of drug and alcohol abuse is unforgiving. Every year she dreams about singing in the show, but no one has taken her on. As you can see, she's hard to take."

"She had a magnificent voice, though."

"Yes, but she stuck with the drugs to the end. She said one day that she'd rather die than go back to prison. She's won—there's no prison here...although it's one immense prison, since we can't leave the limits of New York.

"Might she have been linked to Lennon's disappearance?"

"Possibly. I mentioned the names that I got: they're jazz musicians, who probably didn't want to concert run by an Englishman and film star. I know the subway station where they're holding a battle."

"A what?"

"A battle: two musicians or singers perform in turn before admirers. Charlie Parker started it. One day, he heard a street musician playing in the subway. He got out his sax and joined in. That gave others the idea, and it helps them to pass the time. The days are long, you know, so we occupy them as best we can.

.

Puisqu'à l'heure où Broadway s'agite.
Nous dansons sur le toit.
Du 218 a Dam street.
Moi Robert, toi Lisa.
Qu'importe, New York, New York si ta voix porte.
Sur le Pont de Brooklyn, ma Petite Amoureuse
défie les buildings, comme une enfant teigneuse.

Alex Beaupain, *Brooklyn Bridge.*

[Since Broadway's busy at this hour
We're dancing on the roof
From Two-One-Eight to Dam Street
Me, Robert, you Lisa.
What does New York, New York matter if your voice carries.
Over Brooklyn Bridge, my little lover
challenge the buildings like a wailing child.

Alex Beaupain, *Brooklyn Bridge*.]

They left Madison Square Garden and plunged into Penn Station. Lisa noticed that the corridors were despairingly empty; sometimes they passed a man or a woman with a vacant expression, who didn't look at them. They arrived on the platform and waited for the train. Lisa noticed that she couldn't smell anything, as if the place had been completely sterilized.

They boarded the train, and Lisa saw that it was empty. She was surprised; she had never seen an empty subway train in New York, even at four o'clock in the morning—for the subway ran around the clock seven days a week. Like the city, it only stopped during storms, when water flooded the tunnels.

They finally arrived at Chambers Street. They left the train, and heard distant music. They followed the sound and emerged into a hall in the station in which about a hundred people were assembled, surrounding two saxophonists.

"The one on the right is Charlie Parker."

Bird, thought Lisa, remembering the movie that Clint Eastwood had made about him.

"He died of a drug overdose in New York too, in 1955. He's still here."

"And the other?"

"I don't know. Doubtless an amateur."

Lisa leaned on the wall and listened. The two musicians were competing in virtuousity. She noticed that Chrlie Parker wasn't trying to crush his adversary of a day; on the contrary, he was trying to bring out the best in him. The duel became a veritable duo, the two musicians letting themselves go completely, and Lisa savored the moment of true joy. Once again, she understood that she couldn't rid herself of music, as she had thought for years.

They finished with a frenetic finale, and the applause crackled. Charlie Parker hugged the other musician and congratulated him. Peter and Lisa went to meet them.

"Hi," said Lisa. "Great fingering; I'd have loved to accompany you on the piano."

The two men looked to her in astonishment. "You ain't dead?" said Charlie Parker.

"No, I'm alive—but I can still play the piano."

"What you doin' here? You ain't come to listen to me play just for the pleasure."

"No," Lisa replied, looking his straight in the eyes. "I'm in your world to find John Lennon, so that he can put on his show."

A small ironic smile appeared on Charlie Parker's face.

"I'm the one who brought her," said Peter. "It's not every day that a phantom disappears like that."

"And you think we—we jazzmen—are responsible?"

"The idea had occurred to me," said Lisa dryly.

"Black man abductin' a white musician out of jealousy?" said Charlie Parker. "The police ain't changed since my day. After me, you'll go see the rappers, more blacks."

"You're mistaken," said Peter. "Black or white, it doesn't matter. What's serious is the disappearance of one of ours. Imagine that it might only be the start, that we'll al evaporate one by one."

"So much the better—I approve. If someone has the power, he can start with me. I had enough of being in this city. If I go to hell it don't matter much, but here I can't do no more. So no, I didn' make Lennon disappear. If I'd had the possibility, I'd have started with me. Anyway, I liked the guy. He has good ideas for songs and he's sympatico. You can go look elsewhere. I had nothin' to do with it."

Lisa turned to the other saxophonist, who raised his arms to the heavens, brandishing his instrument. "Likewise. Believe me, I had nothing against John. On the contrary—I was due to play with him at the concert."

Lisa hesitated momentarily. She looked at the two men and said: "You don't have any ideas about this disappearance?"

The two saxophonists shook their heads.

"Thanks," she said, a little put out.

As she turned away, Charlie Parker said: "If you ever find yourself back here, I'll have a jam session with you—we can find you a piano."

Lisa replied, with a smile: "I hope that'll be as late as possible."

Hearty laughter accompanied Lisa and Peter into the corridor.

"We're back where we started," said Peter, "and time's running out."

Lisa went forward, her features drawn. She headed for the stairways that led to the open air. They came out into the Wall Street district. Peter dared not speak; he could see that Lisa was thinking hard and didn't want to interrupt her train of thought. Eventually, they arrived at the statue of George Washington and sat down on the steps.

"There's something escaping me," said Lisa, suddenly. "I have the impression that we've been on the wrong track from the start."

"I'm sorry, but I can't help you any more. I thought it as a matter of rivalry among musicians. You think Sid, Charlie and the rest are innocent?"

"Yes. Charlie put his finger on the essential point: if one of them had found the means to kill a phantom he's have committed suicide." She turned toward Peter and looked him straight in the eyes. "You first."

Peter hesitated before replying.

"Don't tell me ay different," Lisa continued. "I can read it in your face. This is no life, if I can put it that way."

"You're right—we all have suicidal impulses, but it's impossible for us: death, true death, is inaccessible to us. Perhaps it is hell here, not purgatory. But that doesn't solve our problem."

"You're mistaken. If John Lennon hasn't been killed, he's been abducted, or he's disappeared of his own accord. We're going back to Madison Square Garden. I want to see the place again. I must have missed something."

She got to her feet and went down the steps. Peter followed her.

"Can't we take a taxi?" she asked. "I don't want to go back into the subway—it gives me the willies."

"No problem—some phantom driver will see us. We might have to wait a little longer than in your world."

A cab stopped after two minutes. They got into the back and Peter asked for Madison Square Garden.

"I understand now it works with the subway," said Lisa. "You take the same trains as the living, but you don't see them and they can't see you—but I don't get it with the taxis. Why do phantoms continue to drive them?"

"Because they don't know how to do anything else," Peter replied. "Spending hours sitting on a bench in front of the Statue of Liberty only works for a day. At least they have a purpose—driving phantoms, talking to them. I don't have anything; I spend my days walking around. The artists are probably the luckiest ones—they can continue with their art."

"That's not what Charlie Parker thought."

"Let's just say that it's the idea I had—but perhaps it's hard for them."

Téléphone de la cabine
J'te présenterai ma frangine cocaïne
Viens becqueter dans ma cuisine
Tu goûteras à ma copine protéine
Si tu swing dans le timing
T'auras droit aux multivitamines
New York, New York, New York...

Si tu es dans la détresse
J'te présenterai une gonzesse qui caresse
Qui t'fait cracher tes dollars
A peu près comme un tubard ses kleenex
Si t'es pas dans le tempo
Elle t'éponge, et puis ciao, ça presse
New York, New York, New York...

Bernard Lavilliers, *Rock City.*

[Telephone in the booth
This is my woman cocaine
Come have a bit in my kitchen
You can taste my pal protein
If we swing with the rhythm
You'll have multivitamins by right
New York, New York, New York…

If you're in distress
I'll introduce you to a gal's caress
That'll make you spit dollars
Just like a box of Kleenex
If you don't have the rhythm
She'll sponge you, and ciao, hurry up
New York, New York, New York…

Bernard Lavilliers, *Rock City*.]

"Stop!" howls Lisa, suddenly.

The cab pulled up immediately; at least there was no one behind it to blast his horn. Lisa got out and stood in the middle of the street momentarily. She was at the corner of Seventh Avenue and Thirty-Third Street. Peter got out in his turn and joined her. He looked in the same direction and saw the Houdini Museum.

"Is Houdini among the phantoms of New York?" she asked.

"I don't know," said Peter. "I don't know them all. There must be millions of them. Why that question?"

Lisa did not reply. She crossed the street, not without having looked left and right mechanically, and went into the museum, followed by Peter, who asked the cab-driver to wait for them. The place was empty. She stopped in front of a coffin from which Harry Houdini had escaped in 1907 when he had been handcuffed, after having responded to an invitation from the organizers of the Boston marathon. It had only taken him sixty-six minutes to complete the endeavor.

They continued to visit the different rooms without meeting any wandering souls. It was a museum dedicated to the greatest of magicians, as it proclaimed. Lisa studied the clothes and the posters, and an idea began to take form in her mind.

"Lennon isn't dead," she said, in front of a portrait of the famous magician."You think he's still here, among us."

"If I follow your logic and Charlie Parker's, then yes. You've told me that a phantom can't die, so I think it's either an abduction or a voluntary disappearance."

"There were hundreds of people present in the arena, and he was alone on stage. He disappeared just like *that*."

"The spotlights deflected attention. Look here: Houdini was capable of escaping even when shut in a coffin, so he could easily have made Lennon disappear. And there must be more opportunities on the stage of Madison Square Garden than anywhere else for a magician to work his tricks."

"But for what motive?"

"There you're asking me too much. It would be necessary to find Houdini and ask him. But I can't do anything—you're the one who can do that."

Peter laughed briefly. "Phantoms don't appear on video cameras, and there are far fewer dead cops than living ones to look for him. I don't even have a radio or anything—there's jut the two of us."

Lisa looked at her watch. It was nearly midnight. The sun would be rising in almost six hours. A few hours to find the magician, who might be hiding anywhere in New York.

"If nothing happens, it's not serious," said Peter. "At least we know that we're still immortal. Whether Lennon has disappeared or been kidnapped, it's our problem; at least I'm reassured. If we can ever drop the investigation, we can profit from the time we have left to walk and chat before I take you back to the departure point."

Lisa hesitated, but ended up saying: "No, now I've started, I want to go on to the end and find the solution."

"You're like your father—a real pit-bull, who never lets go."

"Yes, even if we only have five hours. I'd like to know the end of the story. You really don't know where we can lay our hands on Houdini?"

"Frankly, no."

"Let's begin by searching the museum. There might be a hidden room here—that would be just like him.

They looked in all the corners, taped all the walls and opened al the cupboards, but they failed to find any hiding place or any clue. Lisa was not surprised; a magician never divulged his tricks. And still there was no phantom presence.

"It's amusing," said Lisa. "I read that all his life, Houdini pursued spiritualists, considering them to be crooks. He didn't believe that the dead could come back to talk to the living. It must have been funny for him to find himself in this world."

"He was right; we can't have any contact with you, except during Manhattanhenge—and then only one person at a time."

"We won't find anything here," said Lisa, fatalistically. "At any rate, if Houdini had abducted Lennon, he wouldn't keep him prisoner in his museum."

The left the place and got back into the taxi.

"Thanks for waiting for us," said Lisa, mechanically.

The driver laughed briefly, and replied: "I have all eternity in front of me, so a few minutes more s nothing. Where are we going? A tour of New York by night?"

"No, Madison Square Garden, as was our original intention."

"You want to watch the rehearsal?" said the driver, as he accelerated. "I hope it'll be better than last year—it must be said that I'm no fan of opera, but it practically put me to sleep."

"It's possible that there won't be a concert this year."

"Why?"

While Peter explained the situation, Lisa looked out of the window. It really was New York that she was seeing, but a New York in slow motion, a cinematic New York. She remembered and video shot by an amateur who had filmed the streets and avenues empty, with no cars and no people. She had wondered how he had been able to do that. For her, New York was synonymous with intense life.

Peter's voice pulled her out of her reverie.

"We've arrived."

As they opened the car door Peter saw Edgar Allan Poe leaving Madison Square Garden. A sudden idea crossed her mind. She said to the driver, in a tone that brooked no protest: "Take us to the Dakota Building."

"No problem—you're the boss."

Peter stared at Lisa and said: "Why there?"

"An idea. I'll explain when we get there."

"Hang on, if I'm thinking right, you want to see the apartment where John Lennon lived.?"

"Have you read the Poe short story in which everyone is looking for a compromising letter?"

"No. It means nothing to me. You know…reading and me…."

"The police are searching for a letter that must be hidden in an apartment. They've searched everywhere, sounded everything, but found nothing. A detective arrives who reasons differently and understands that the letter hasn't been hidden, but rather put in an obvious place by the guilty party. He discovers it folded up with a another letter and placed backwards. It was in plain view, but the police thought it was unimportant."

"You think that John Lennon is there."

"I don't know, I'm looking. Time's against us, so we have to move fast and follow all the trails."

Standing on the corner
Just me and Yoko Ono
We was waiting for Jerry to land
Up come a man with the guitar in his hand
Singing "Have a marijuana if you can"
His name was Davis Peel
And we found that he was real
He sang "The pope smokes dope everyday"
Up come a police man shoved us up the street
Singing, "Power to the people today!"
NYC...NYC...NYC
Que pasa NY?...Que pasa NY?

John Lennon, *New York City*.

The Dakota Building stands at the north-western corner of Seventy-Second Street and Central Park West. Its construction was completed in 1884. It was built around a courtyard, and in that era its entrance door could let a coach and horses through. Its apartments had sold out quickly because, for well-to-do New Yorkers, it was fashionable to live in that kind of tall building. Lisa remembered that it had been the skyscraper in the Polanski film *Rosemary's Baby*. She smiled on thinking she wouldn't be with the Devil, but with phantoms. It was, above all, the building in front of which John Lennon had been murdered.

On the other side of the street, at the entrance to Central Park, Yoko Ono had had a memorial built dedicated to her husband, the Strawberry Field. It had the form of a triangle, the heart of which was constituted by symbols representing peace and in the center the word IMAGINE, the title of one of his most famous songs. Since then, numerous admirers had gathered there, singing and placing flowers and candles.

Lisa looked at the building; she had contemplated it countless times, but had never been able to get inside, that privilege being reserved for residents and their guests.

"Can you find out where John Lennon's apartment is?" she asked.

"It shouldn't be a problem—it's his wife's. Come with me; we'll get in without any problem."

"You're right; I still thought that I was in my world, but here there aren't any doormen to stop me going in."

It was with some slight apprehension that she crossed the threshold, bat no one ran forward to drive her back. Peter looked at the directory of residents and took her up to Yoko Ono's apartment.

"How are we going to get in?" she said, pausing outside the door, her arms dangling.

Peter smiled.

"You're no longer in your world. Even if the door's locked in that one and Yoko Ono isn't at home, everything is open here. If there's anyone there, it will be a phantom. You're the only living person in this city, for a few more hours."

Lisa turned the handle, and the door opened without the slightest difficult. She went inside, followed by Peter.

She arrived in an immense room with a stone fireplace in the center. Exposed brickwork, high ceilings and wooden beams were combined with vast white walls and wooden floorboards. But the apartment was empty: not a single item of furniture, nothing that revealed any human presence.

"You're sure this is the right one? It doesn't look as if anyone lives here."

"Yes, it's definitely John Lennon's apartment—perhaps Yoko Ono has moved."

They advanced into the immense empty room and stopped. Facing them, sitting in an armchair, a man was fixing them with a hypnotic gaze. Lisa took a fraction of a second to recognize Houdini. He hadn't changed; he was the same as on the posters and photograph in his museum.

"Hello, Mr. Houdini," she said, moving closer to him. "Would you care to tell us where you're keeping John Lennon prisoner?"

"I don't know how you worked it out, but you've succeeded. It's not worth the trouble of lying to you—he's here, locked in the bathroom on the far side of the room. Are you going to arrest me and put me in prison?" Houdini emitted a loud burst of laughter. "Already," he went on, "when I was human, no prison, coffin or straitjacket could hold me for long; now that I'm a phantom, you can't do anything to me."

Lisa went past him without replying. She opened the bathroom door. He was there, sitting on the ground, looking at her behind his little round glasses. He was still so young. Lisa felt a lump in her throat. John Lennon was at her feet, and she could find the words to speak to him.

"You're free," she stammered. "If you want, we can take you to Madison Square Garden. They're waiting for you to prepare the show."

John Lennon got up and tried to hug Lisa, but passed through her. The young woman couldn't help smiling on seeing the artist's disconcerted expression.

"But you're alive!"

"Yes," said Lisa, "and permit me to tell you that you're one of the greatest musicians ever, and that I've always admired you. When I can, I play your songs in a bar, especially the one about New York, and *Imagine*, of course." She had said that without thinking. When she had finished, she thought it ridiculous—quite ridiculous. "Excuse me—I'm overwhelmed by being here in front of you. A little while ago, I found myself in front of Marilyn Monroe."

"How is she?" asked Lennon.

"She's waiting for you, to sing with you."

Lisa drew him into the room where Peter and Houdini were. When she came level with him, Lisa couldn't help asking the magician: "Why the abduction?"

"Because it's only for the musicians," snapped Houdini. "Every year it's the same. The show's reserved for musicians, not other artists. We don't exist—we're nothing. Thousands of people witnessed my exploits, but today, because I don't sing, because I don't play an instrument, I'm good for nothing. I've been forgotten. And to be forgotten is the worst thing there is for a phantom. Even my museum is empty. So, this year, I decided to strike a great blow. I was going to show that I'm an artist, a true one. During the show, I was going to appear on the stage, and make John Lennon appear in a spectacular fashion…."

He stopped and looked at the three faces. He pulled a face and hurled at them: "How can two policemen and an adulated star understand my art? Are you going to arrest me? No? In that case, I'll go—and good luck with your show, but don't expect me to listen to it!"

"Wait!" said John Lennon. "You're right, we've thought too much about ourselves. Why not put on a show with all the arts? Ask dancers to create a ballet around our music, painters to decorate the stage, circus artistes to join us on stage. We still have a few more days to organize it."

"Are you serious?" asked Houdini.

"As serious as can be. I'm even getting more ideas."

"All right," said Houdini. "I'm your man."

John Lennon turned to Lisa and said: "Thanks for having rescued me. If I can ever do anything for you…."

Lisa held her breath, and let it out in one go. "I still have four hours before going back to my world. If I could hear you sing jut once…I wasn't even born in time to see you in concert to Madison Square Garden. And if I dared…."

"Dare!"

"I'd like to accompany you on the piano while you sing *New York City*."

"Let's go to the Madison right away. Let's not waste any time." He turned to Houdini and asked: "Are you coming with us?"

"Of course!"

While they headed toward the apartment door, Peter asked Houdini: "Why did you hide him here?"

"Simple—it was Poe who gave me the idea, by talking about his stories. I told myself that no one would look here—and I thought it had worked…but no."

Peter turned to Lisa and raised his thumb, nodding his head.

Start spreading the news,
I'm leaving today
I wanna be a part of it,
New York, New York.

Frank Sinatra, *New York New York*

Lisa could not get over it. She had played the piano while John Lennon sang. After that, it had been Marilyn Monroe who had wanted to sing while she played. Then Charlie Parker had passed by and had jammed with her, as promised. Even Billie Holliday had wanted to show that her voice had lost none of its presence, in spite of the drugs, the alcohol and death. Lisa had never had such a golden moment. Then Peter had come to look for her because the time was approaching when she had to go back. She said goodbye to John Lennon and thanked him for the moment that would remain engraved in her memory forever.

As she left Madison Square Garden Lisa felt a desire to stay in that world. To do that, she would have to commit suicide. She imagined spending her life playing with all those stars, with all the headliners she adored.

Peter must have read the thought on the young woman's face, because he said, in a firm voice: "Don't even think about it. For two hours of happiness you'd be in pain for years. Go back to your world, go on playing for pleasure, bear your cross as best you can…and I know that's not easy."

They took a taxi, which brought them to Fourteenth Street. She got out while he stated inside.

"See you," she murmured.

"Who knows?" he replied, closing the door.

She watched the cab pull away, and closed her eyes.

Un jour j'irai à New-York avec toi
Toutes les nuits déconner
Et voir aucun film en entier, ça va d'soi
Avoir la vie partagée, tailladée
Bercés par le ronron de l'air conditionné
Dormir dans un hôtel délatté
Traîner du côté gay et voir leurs corps se serrer
Voir leurs cœurs se vider et saigner
Oui, saigner

[Refrain]
un jour, j'irai là-bas
un jour, chat, un autre rat
voir si le cœur de la ville bat en toi
et tu m'emmèneras
emmène-moi

Téléphone : *Un jour j'irais à New York avec toi*

Lisa opened her eyes. She found herself at the corner of Fourteenth Street and Eighth Avenue. There were still a few photographers around her. When she turned her head to the right the sun had almost disappeared, swallowed up by the buildings. She took out her phone. It was still the thirtieth of May, and it was 8:32 p.m. She breathed deeply and told herself that she really needed a vacation. However, she remembered all of the adventure she had believed she was living through with the phantoms. She remembered everything, down to the smallest details of the night. Had she imagined it? It was more than probable.

Several people pushed pat her in order to cross the street, without paying the slightest attention to her. She continued breathing slowly in order to get her mind completely straight, and then cross the road in her turn and headed at a rapid pace for the bar where she had to sing.

When she arrived at the door, she hesitated. The story had left its mark on her and she didn't know if she was really in any state to sing that evening. She could say that she was ill; the owner wouldn't hold it against her. Finally, she decided to go in; she would soon find out.

She went in. At least since the anti-smoking law one could breathe in bars—a good idea of the mayor's. She nodded to a few regulars, mostly cops, blew a kiss to the owner and headed for the piano, which was waiting for her.

As she was taking off her coat, she felt something in the right hand pocket. She took it out and saw a wad of paper. She unfolded it, and started trembling as she read what as written on the first page: a simple sentence, written by hand.

For Lisa, to sing in the other world. A present from me.

And an illegible signature.

On the next page were the words of the song about New York written by John Lennon, which he had sung for her. On the other pages was the score.

A waitress set down a bottle of water and a glass, and smiled at her to encourage her.

Lisa let herself fall on to the stool. She put the pages in front of her and her hands waited for the order to proceed, a few millimeters from the keys. She saw the fingers descend upon the keyboard, as if endowed with a life of their own, and the notes spilled out into the bar. She heard herself singing the song, which she had only heard once.

Her high crystalline voice made the last conversations fall silent: a voice that some people compared to a sharp blade, as trenchant as steel. She sang with utter finesse and delicacy, articulating the words perfectly, fitting the rhythm to the chorus. The song bore more resemblance to *Imagine* than *New York City*, but it was a vibrant homage to New York. John Lennon had put all of his soul into it.

She held the last note while her fingers gradually stopped running over the keys.

When she had finished, there was a brief moment of silence, followed by thunderous applause.

Lisa continued with a classic from her standard repertoire, but a part of her mind remained in the New York populated by phantoms.

At one moment, she looked mechanically at the room and one of her fingers slipped on the keyboard, but she recovered immediately, and looked at the keys instead—because facing her, sitting in a corner, in the seats of two policemen, she had just seen John Lennon and Marilyn Monroe smiling at her.

She forced herself to look in their direction again. They were still there, encouraging her by clapping their hands. She smiled at them, and carried on singing.

When she had finished her set, she poured herself a glass of water. She drank it slowly, looking in the direction of the two stars—but in their place, the policemen in civilian dress had reappeared. She told herself that it had all been nothing but a dream, and that even if her adventure had been true, Peter had told her that the living could not see the phantoms, and vice versa. In any case, Manhattanhenge was over.

She called the waitress and asked hr for a glass of bourbon. It was not her habit to drink alcohol, but what the hell—she needed a pick-me-up to chase away the phantoms that were pursuing her.

The waitress came back with the glass, and she immediately emptied it in one gulp. The alcohol burned her palate. She felt a gentle warmth rising from her stomach. She set the glass down on the piano, turned her head and saw a man standing in front of her.

He was of medium height, shorter than her, white, dressed in expensive clothes, doubtless made to measure. Lisa looked down; the shoes were similar. She looked back at the face: nothing remarkable, except for a tiny dimple in the chin; a seductive appearance, seemingly sure of himself, with an undeniable charm that ought to please the ladies.

"You have a magnificent voice and an ethereal touch."

"Thanks," she said, sighing to imply that the line was familiar and that she had heard it a hundred times before.

"I didn't know the first song you sang. Is it yours?"

Lisa hesitated, unsure as to what to reply. Then she murmured: "No, it was written by a friend who died a long time ago. I decided to sing it for the first time tonight as a tribute to him."

The man stared at her intently, and a smile appeared on his face. "You've seen them, then," he said.

"Who?" asked Lisa, intrigued.

"The ghosts of Manhattan."

www.ingramcontent.com/pod-product-compliance
Lightning Source LLC
Chambersburg PA
CBHW040958170626
46815CB00002B/66